The Tiger who lost his Stripes

STORY BY ANTHONY PAUL

PICTURES BY MICHAEL FOREMAN

SPARROW
BOOKS

A Sparrow Book

Published by Arrow Books Limited

17-21 Conway Street, London W1P 6JD

An imprint of the Hutchinson Publishing Group
London Melbourne Sydney Auckland Johannesburg
and agencies throughout the world

First published by Andersen Press 1980
Sparrow edition 1983

Text © Anthony Paul 1980
Illustrations © Michael Foreman 1980

Printed and bound in Great Britain by
Blantyre Printing & Binding Ltd, London and Glasgow

ISBN 09 932070 3

Of all the animals in the forest the most magnificent was General MacTiger.
He had fierce flashing eyes, a handsome bristling face, and a most stately
walk. But most splendid of all was his coat. It was honey-golden, licorice-
black, as thick and silky as a Persian rug, and dazzlingly striped.

But one morning General MacTiger woke up feeling odd. So he went to look at his reflection in the river. His eyes looked bright. His tongue looked pink. His whiskers bristled properly. Yet there was something wrong. He stared at his reflection for some time before he saw what that was; and when he did, he could hardly believe his eyes. He was all yellow! His stripes had gone!

This must be a dream, he thought. So he said, "All right, that's enough of that—time to wake up and get on with the day's serious business." (General MacTiger was an enormously important tiger who was always getting on with serious business.) But now he found he couldn't wake up because, of course, he was already awake. So he had to admit that somehow or other he had lost his stripes.

How do you think he behaved? Did he say to himself, "How careless of me; ah well, I suppose I shall just have to manage without them"? Indeed he did not. Tigers take themselves and their stripes very seriously. A tiger's whole tigerishness is in his stripes.

Did he sit down and cry? Certainly not. A tiger never cries.

Did he get into a fearful rage, and snort like a boiling steam-engine? Did he roar till the trees trembled? Well, he nearly did; but he stopped, remembering that he was General MacTiger, and must always be dignified and stately.

So he kept calm, and said to himself, "By George, what a remarkable case of stripelessness! I must get to the bottom of it." So he felt more like himself. Then he set off to look for the stripes, trying to look as if nothing was wrong.

But he looked very odd. The other animals watched him pass, and their eyes grew round and their fur stood on end and they muttered to one another, "General MacTiger has lost his stripes; he is all yellow." They slunk back into their dens to think about this strange business.

General MacTiger looked in the long grass, in the reeds, in the bamboo groves. He even looked in pitch-dark caves. Nothing. Not a sniff or a whisper of those stripes could he find.

After hours of searching, General MacTiger plodded home. By now he didn't feel at all like himself. Even his growl sounded oddly croaky. And what if he tried to roar and it came out wrong, as a honk or a hoot? It was too awful to think about. Perhaps he had been changed into quite a different animal, some yellow stranger? This thought made him feel most unhappy.

Trudging sadly along, he came to a clearing in the forest. There in the middle, hanging from a branch, was something that had not been there before. It was a sort of bag or basket woven out of strips of dark stuff. It looked something like a wasp's nest, something like a hammock, something like a long sock. General MacTiger stood staring at it, and, as he stared, anger built up inside him like steam in a pressure-cooker, until it burst out in a truly tremendous crackling roar.

"MY STRIPES!" roared General MacTiger.

From the basket-thing slid a flat head on the end of a long neck that wasn't a neck. It was the head of the python. In a dry whispery voice like a sleeve caught in barbed wire, the python said, "Would you mind making less noise?"

"Fury! Roar! Hijacker!" thundered the General.

"There's no point in this fuss and foolishness," said the python. "I never give anything up once I've got my hands on it."

"But you haven't got any hands," said General MacTiger.

"So what?" whispered the python, and slid back inside the basket-thing.

After a minute or so the General made a much smaller roar, more like a cough. The python said, "I'm trying to digest a goat, and I wish you'd stop disturbing me. You're as noisy as a motorbike."

"What do you know about motorbikes?" said the General. "There are no motorbikes in the forest."

"That's one of the reasons I live here," said the python. "I can't stand the noise of motorbikes."

"The point is," said the General, "what are you doing in there?"

"I've told you," sneered the python. "I'm *trying* to digest my dinner."

"Stop trying to snake your way out of it, snake," said the General. "I mean, how dare you take my stripes?"

The python shrugged. It's hard to shrug without shoulders, but the python managed.

"Look, if you don't give me back those stripes—" said the General.

"What?" said the python.

"—I shall get very angry indeed!"

"How terrifying!" said the python. "Let me know in advance, so that I can put my ear-plugs in. I do hate loud noises."

General MacTiger made a choking sound like water going down the plughole. Then, before he had time to stop himself, he said, "But you haven't got any ears!"

"And you haven't got any stripes," said the python. "And pretty silly you look without them."

The python slid back inside the basket-thing, leaving General MacTiger just opening and closing his mouth.

When General MacTiger had had a good think he called out, "Hey, python!"

"What is it now?" said the python.

"So you aren't going to give me my stripes back?"

"Tiger," said the python. "You are not so stupid as you look."

General MacTiger paid no attention to this. He said, "What do you want in exchange for my stripes?"

"Well, I like this house," said the python. "But I suppose if you could build me an even better one...."

"What sort of better one?"

"Oh, a good strong one of branches, elephant grass, that sort of thing."

"Elephant grass!" said General MacTiger. "How can I build a house of elephant grass?"

"Perhaps the elephants will help you," said the python, and slid back inside his nest.

General MacTiger found the elephants in the river, having splashy heavy fun. Being so large, the elephants weren't afraid to laugh at anyone, and when they saw him they laughed heartily. "You do look comic," they shouted, "you've forgotten to put your football jersey on. Ho ho!"

General MacTiger thought that even without stripes he was far handsomer than the elephants with their great cabbagey ears and the bits of hosepipe they wore stuck onto the fronts of their faces. But this was no time to say so.

Instead, he smiled politely and said, "I wonder if you could help me? I'm building a house for a friend... it's the sort of job you fellows could do in a few minutes, I expect...."

"Hmm," said the Chief Elephant. "Who is this fine present for?"

"Well actually," said the General, "it's for a snake I know. The—er—python."

The Chief Elephant trumpeted and tromboned; bunches of bananas thumped down from the trees. He wobbled all over with elephant-sized laughter. "The tiger wants to make a house for his dear friend the python!" he shouted; and all the elephants trumpeted and tuba'd, and spouted water at one another. Because the elephants knew that the python had *no* friends; especially not the tiger.

"Very funny, I know," said General MacTiger. "But you see the python has my stripes—you've noticed I'm not wearing them today—and he won't give them back until I make him a house. If you help me, perhaps I could do something in return...."

The General couldn't think of anything he could do for the elephants; but the Chief Elephant said, "There is something you can do for us. We have a small problem: the crocodiles have been straying into our part of the river, and one or two of our younger members have had nasty bites in the ankles. If you're such friends with the python you're probably pally with the crocodiles too; no doubt they'll do whatever you ask!"

Then, slurping and sloshing, the elephants heaved themselves out of the river and trampled off into the forest.

Standing well up on the riverbank, General MacTiger called down to
the Grandmother of All the Crocodiles, who lay in the water as still as a log,
with one pebbly eye open.

"Look here," said the General, importantly, "you crocodiles have got to
stay out of the elephants' part of the river, do you hear?"

The Grandmother of All the Crocodiles said, "Why?" Her voice was something between a deep burp and the creaking of rusty hinges.

At first General MacTiger couldn't think of a good answer. But then he thought, and said, "Well, you know what elephants are—great clumsy things. They're afraid that if you get too close to them you may get trodden on."

The General felt cunning and pleased with himself at thinking of this.

The Grandmother of All the Crocodiles looked at him without blinking for quite a long time. Then she said, "If the elephants are so worried about treading on us, why don't *they* move?"

The General had no answer ready; so he blustered, "Oh—well—they don't want to, and that's that."

The Grandmother of All the Crocodiles croaked, "And if we move, what do we get?"

"Well you won't get trodden on," said General MacTiger.

"That's something we shan't get," said the Grandmother of All the Crocodiles, grinning like a bear-trap. "But what *shall* we get?"

"Oh doom and despair," thought the General, "where will this business end?"

Now the Grandmother of All the Crocodiles thought, in her secret stony self, that it might not be a bad idea to move out of the elephants' part of the river. But crocodiles are unhelpful; and just because they had been asked to move, she thought they might stay. At any rate, they wouldn't move for nothing.

"I know," said the Grandmother of All the Crocodiles. "We *may* move if you can deal with the monkeys."

"Monkeys?" said the General.

"Yes. They drop coconuts on us. They think it's a great joke."

And at that very moment down came a shower of coconuts, bonk bonk bonk, one to each crocodile. "You see?" said the Grandmother of All the Crocodiles. "Get these monkeys to stop their monkey tricks, or we stay put." And she fell silent and lay still, as if to make it clear that when a crocodile stays put, it really stays put.

"Fine," said General MacTiger, and bounded away. But he didn't know
how he was going to manage this. Getting monkeys to behave themselves is
like catching the wind in a paper bag, like teaching parrots to think for
themselves. To begin with, he couldn't even see them: monkeys always keep
well out of the way when tigers are around.

"Monkeys, are you there?" called General MacTiger.

A shower of nuts and ripe fruit landed on him, so he knew the monkeys were up there.

"Good," said the General, wiping himself clean. (He didn't have to swallow his anger, because he had got so used to swallowing it he thought he must have swallowed it for good.) "Now listen, monkeys—" But now the monkeys started such a chattering that he couldn't hear his own words, and had to stop. Actually, he didn't know what to say next anyway.

But now he had a chance to think; and when the monkeys' noise had died down a bit, he said to himself, "Let me see if my thinking is right", and he called out, "Monkeys! Be quiet a moment—I have something important to say."

Straight away the monkeys started up again, louder than ever.

When the monkeys had grown tired of making so much noise, the General shouted, "Monkeys! Where are you? I can't hear you any more!"

And when they heard this the monkeys shut up completely. The silence was amazing. Never had there been such a silence in the forest: it was so silent that other creatures stopped what they were doing to listen to the silence. The bears, boars and baboons stopped rooting and rummaging in the bushes and rocks. Bees and beetles stopped buzzing and droning. The elephants stood like stone elephants, holding bundles of grass in their trunks halfway to their open mouths.

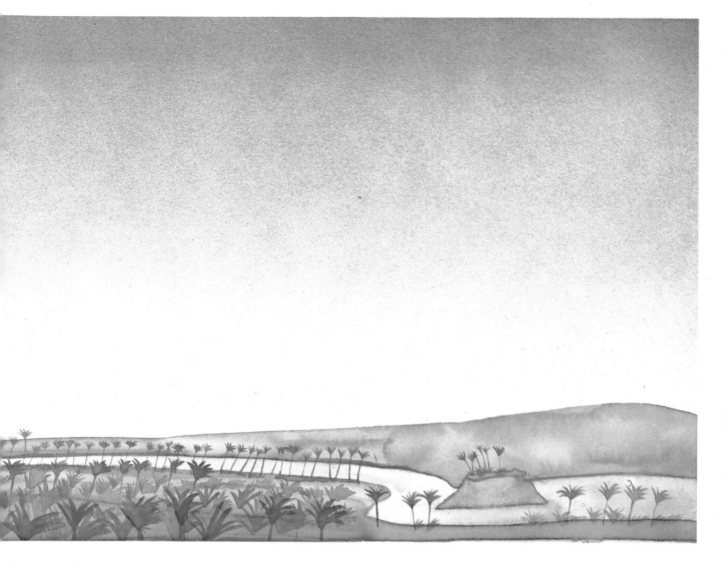

It was the most unnatural and unearthly silence.

Eventually there fell into this silence a small dry noise. It was the sound of General MacTiger laughing. Then gradually the other forest noises started up again.

"Monkeys!" cried General MacTiger. "I have come from the crocodiles to thank you for your kind gifts of coconuts. Please send them more, as many as you can manage. They love coconuts. Thank you, kind monkeys."

General MacTiger went and told the crocodiles that the monkeys would not drop any more coconuts on them. The Grandmother of All the Crocodiles opened her other eye and said, "How did you manage it?"

"Oh," said General MacTiger, "once you understand the monkeys they aren't so difficult."

So the crocodiles moved out of the elephants' water.

General MacTiger went to the elephants and said, "You see? The crocodiles have moved."

The Chief Elephant made a noise like air escaping from bagpipes. "How did you manage it?" he said.

"Oh," said General MacTiger. "When you get to know the crocodiles they aren't so crusty."

So the elephants broke off branches and pulled up elephant grass, and built a hut-thing. General MacTiger went to the python and said, "There's your new house. Now give me back my stripes."

The python looked at the hut-thing, saw that it was strong and neatly made, and slithered into it, letting General MacTiger's stripes fall in a tangle to the ground.

Quick as a flash, General MacTiger untangled the stripes and put them back on.

Now he felt tigerish again, and roared happily, and capered about like an enormous kitten, before he remembered that he was General MacTiger, and must always be dignified and stately.

So he became extremely stately, and roamed through the forest making sure that everything was as it should be.